Teaching practice

Some Romani words used in this book

chavvis	children
Gaujo	non-Gypsy
koshter	clothes pegs
kushti	good
Romani	Gypsy
vardo	wagon

The author and publishers would like to thank Lee and his family, Mr S. McClew, Gypsy Liaison Officer in Berkshire, Mr D.C. Griffiths, Headmaster, and the staff at Waltham St Lawrence School, Berkshire, for making this book possible.

The picture on page 4 is reproduced by permission of the John Topham Picture Library. The wagon on page 5 is part of the collection at the Romany Folklore Museum and Workshop in Selborne, Hampshire. The illustration on page 6 is by Kate Rogers.

First published in Great Britain 1985 by
Hamish Hamilton Children's Books
Garden House, 57–59 Long Acre, London WC2E 9JZ
Copyright © 1985 by Hamish Hamilton (text)
Copyright © 1985 by Hamish Hamilton (photographs)

British Library Cataloguing in Publication Data
Patterson, José
A Traveller Child.
1. Gypsies——Great Britain——Social life
and customs——Juvenile literature
I. Title   II. Taylor, Liba
941'.00491497   DX211
ISBN 0-241-11573-6

Printed in Great Britain by
Cambus Litho, East Kilbride

A TRAVELLER CHILD

José Patterson

Photographs by Liba Taylor

Hamish Hamilton
London

There are many kinds of Traveller people all over the world. Long ago, travelling tinkers mended pots and pans. Travelling salesmen were called pedlars. Gypsies, or Romanies, were famous for buying and selling horses and telling fortunes. Many still do so today. Some Gypsies speak their own language called Romani.

Gypsies, or Travellers, used to live in beautifully painted horse-drawn wagons called vardos. At the end of the day, the family collected wood for a fire. The food was put in a big pot. This was hung over the fire on a metal hook called a kettle iron. There aren't many vardos in use today. Modern Travellers prefer to drive lorries and cars.

4

Some Travellers lived in 'bender tents'. A few even live in them today. A bender tent is made by bending branches of hazel wood into the shape of a barrel. This is covered with cloths and blankets. In summer, it is warm and comfortable; in winter, it is very cold.

Today, many Travellers live in modern caravans or trailers.
Morecoombe, Arrow, Astral, Selborne and Sovereign are the names
of some of the bigger ones. Thomson Sprite and Cavalier are two of
the smaller ones.

A small generator supplies electricity for the television and lighting.
Calor gas is used for cooking and heating. Some trailers have coal
fires. There is no running water, and churns are used to store water.
They are kept clean and shining. A quiet place with clean water,
which is near to the shops, is hard to find. Travellers are not always
allowed to stay in one place for long, and are told to move on.

This is Lee. He is a Traveller boy, and is ten years old. Lee loves playing football and riding his bicycle. He likes performing tricks on his bicycle.

Lee, his sister Teresa, and his Mum and Dad live on a permanent site for Traveller families. They used to live in an Astral trailer which could be towed by the family lorry. Now they live in a mobile home, or chalet as it is sometimes called. It was built in two halves, and is 10 metres long and 7 metres wide. It is too big to be towed. It has three bedrooms, a sitting-room, bathroom and kitchen. It has electricity and running water.

Lee's Dad is called Ted. He works hard collecting scrap metal. The scrap is sorted into different kinds of metals and sold. Ted is repairing a piece of metal pipe.

At other times, Ted might chop down trees, or sell Christmas trees. Sometimes, he lays a tarmac path. Whatever work he does, he likes to be his own boss. He does not want to work for Gaujos. 'Jobs are hard to find,' Ted says. 'I sometimes have to travel a long way to get work.'

Here are Phyllis and George,
Lee's Grandma and Grandad.
Lee calls George 'Grandfa'.
They live in a chalet next door.
Phyllis is very proud of her
beautiful Aynsley china.

When George was a young man,
he liked to paint pretty
patterns on his wagon.
'You need a steady hand not to
smudge the paint,' he says. He
needs more time to sit and
rest now. But now and then,
he helps Ted with his work.

Lee often pops in to see Phyllis and George. Phyllis tells Lee about the old days.

'When we were chavvis we travelled all the time. My mother and father lived in a vardo. We did not stay in one place long enough to go to school every day, so we did not learn to read and write like you.

'We used to sit round the fire and make wooden and paper flowers. We also made clothes pegs, called koshter. The next day, my mother and I would go from door to door and sell them. With the money we earned, we bought food.'

The wooden flowers are made from elderberry wood. Phyllis is using a special knife for carving the wood. The knife belonged to her mother. It is very sharp. Phyllis ties a scarf round her leg in case the knife slips. The flower has a lovely smell of fresh wood.

When the flower shape is made, it is dipped in a coloured dye and put on a leafy stem. Phyllis proudly displays a big bunch of wooden flowers she has made.

13

Lee is very lucky. He has two Grandmas. This is Angelina, although everyone calls her Nunny. She lives in a small trailer next to Ted and Hilda. She is busy cooking giblet broth and cabbage. She knows this is Lee's favourite meal, and often makes it for him. Like many Travellers, Nunny uses separate bowls for washing dishes and clothes.

Lee often visits Nunny – though not just to eat! He likes to keep her company now she lives alone. Her husband died two years ago.

Lee looks at some old photographs. This one is of Nunny's father, who was a soldier in the First World War.

Traveller children help their families in many ways. In the holidays and at weekends, Lee helps his mother with the shopping. He also helps his father on tarmac jobs. He pushes the wheelbarrow and shovels the tarmac. It is hard work.

Best of all Lee enjoys helping his Dad with the car and lorry. He knows how to check the oil and water levels. Dad shows Lee what has gone wrong with the engine. When Lee is grown up, he will drive the lorry and help Dad with his work.

Ted buys some wood and saws it into pieces. Lee chops up the pieces and puts them in bags. Now he brings the sticks into the chalet for the fire. He chops wood for Phyllis and Nunny too.

This is Rayboy, Lee's little cousin. He has come to stay with Phyllis and George for a few days. Lee plays with Rayboy and watches him all the time. There isn't always a safe place for children to play on the site. Space has to be found to park the family lorry and for scrap to be sorted.

Lee and his family sometimes visit other cousins who live in a house. At the back of the house is a beautiful old wagon which belonged to the grandparents. It has been kept to remind the children how Travellers lived in the old days. Lee climbs on to the wagon.

'It was a slow way to travel, but you did have time to look around you,' he says. 'I can't do that when I am in the lorry with Dad because we go too fast.'

Lee goes to school. He works hard at his lessons. His teacher is talking to the children about their work. She is marking Lee's work book. All the family are pleased that Lee is getting on well.

Lee likes sports best of all. He won a cup at the school sports day for running.

Lee is learning to use the computer. He is writing a story called The Magic Tree.

Here is the first part of his story. Can you read it?

One day after school Lee tells his family about the school Christmas Bazaar. It will be held in the village hall. There will be lots of stalls with gifts for people to buy for Christmas. The money will be used to buy a record player for the school. Lee asks Mum what he can take to sell.

'Ask Phyllis to make some of her pretty flowers,' says Mum. 'I am sure they will sell well.'

Phyllis buys coloured paper, wire and coloured dyes for the flowers.
These will be made out of paper. She shows Lee how to make them
just as his great-grandma did. He pulls and curls the edges of the
paper with a knife to form a petal shape. The paper is then carefully
wound round and round until it looks like a rose.

They work hard and make a lovely big bunch of flowers.

On the morning of the Bazaar, Lee is up early. The flowers are loaded into Nunny's van. Lee and Phyllis drive to the village hall and Phyllis carefully carries them inside.

Everyone is busy getting the hall ready for the Bazaar. There are parcels to unpack, gifts to arrange and balloons to blow up.
'I hope the flowers sell,' Lee says to himself.

Lots of people come to the Bazaar to buy presents for Christmas.
Lee goes to the stall to see how the flowers are selling. There are
only a few left now.

Just before the Bazaar closes, Lee takes one last look at the stall. There is only one flower left!

'Grandma will be pleased', thinks Lee. 'I know exactly what she will say when I tell her. She'll say, "That's kushti – that's good. Well done, young Lee!"'